**Pteranodon**

t-RAN-uh-don

**Deinonychus**

DINE-o-NIKE-us

**Mononykus**

MON-o-NIKE-us

## Diplodocus
dip-LOD-o-kus

## Triceratops
try-SERRA-tops

## Tyrannosaurus
tie-RAN-o-saw-rus

## Kronosaurus
krone-o-SAW-rus

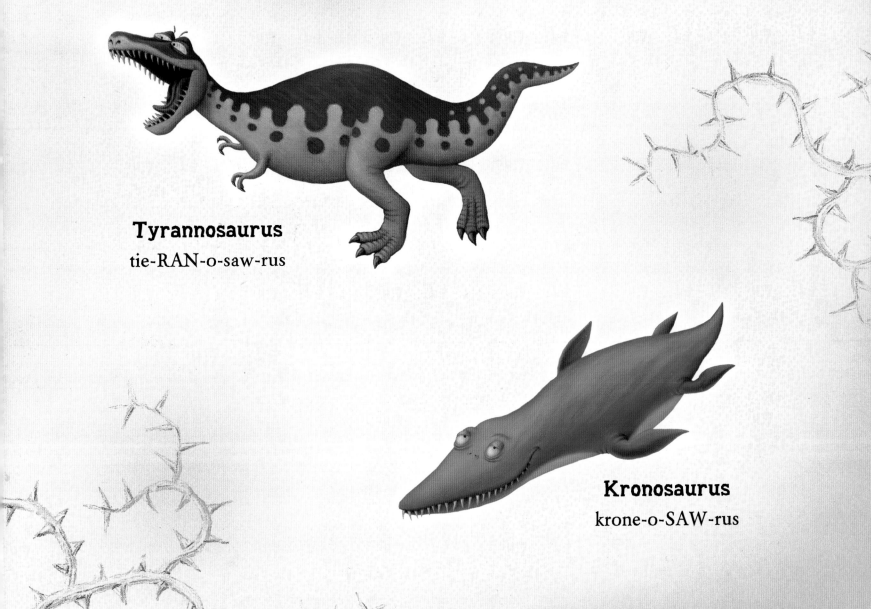

To Joe Luis Young
from Old Tony Mitton
– T.M.

For Fynnjan, and
dinosaur lovers everywhere!
– L.C.

KINGFISHER

First published 2009 by Kingfisher
an imprint of Macmillan Children's Books
a division of Macmillan Publishers Limited
20 New Wharf Road, London N1 9RR
Basingstoke and Oxford
Associated companies throughout the world
www.panmacmillan.com

ISBN: 978 0 7534 1660 0 (HB)
ISBN: 978 0 7534 1843 7 (PB)

Text copyright © Tony Mitton 2009
Illustrations copyright © Lynne Chapman 2009
Moral rights asserted.

www.lynnechapman.co.uk

1 3 5 7 9 10 8 6 4 2

A CIP catalogue record for this book is available from the British Library.

Printed in China
1TR/0309/LFG/UNTD/157MA/C

The website address listed in this book is correct at the time of going to print.
The publisher cannot be held responsible for changes in website addresses or content,
or for information obtained through third party websites.

# Gnash, Gnaw, DINOSAUR!

## Prehistoric poems with lift-the-flap surprises!

Written by
**Tony Mitton**

Illustrated by
**Lynne Chapman**

KINGFISHER

# We lived long ago . . .

We're back in this book with a big hello.
Come and see us moving as we slosh through the swamp.
Come and watch us eating as we chomp, chomp, chomp.
Some of us are massive, and tower up tall.
Some of us are tiny, ever so small.
Some roam the prairie, some swim the sea,
and some ride the breezes, flying round free.
There are many kinds of dinosaur here for you to meet.
So dip into these pages for a dinosaur treat . . .

# Diplodocus

Diplodocus. That's me. Hello.

With my long, lithe neck I can sweep round low.

If I see lush leaves at the top of the trees

I can crane up high and crop them with ease.

But although I am peaceful and plodding and slow,

if you annoy me you'll get a hard blow.

You may think I'm dopey and droopy and dippy,

but watch for my tail as it's long, strong and whippy!

# Pteranodon

I am Pteranodon. Just look at meeeeeeeee!
Sweeping and gliding and flying so freeeeeeeee!

# Tyrannosaurus

I'm Tyrannosaurus. I am the boss.
I'm also the fiercest. So don't get me cross.

Ace hang-glider, air-current rider, clifftop-swooper, keen loop-the-looper - - - - - -
Watch how my leathery wings spread wide,
helping me hover and wheel and glide.
Watch how I whirl from the cliffs with a wheeeeeeeee!
swooping to scoop up a fish from the sea.

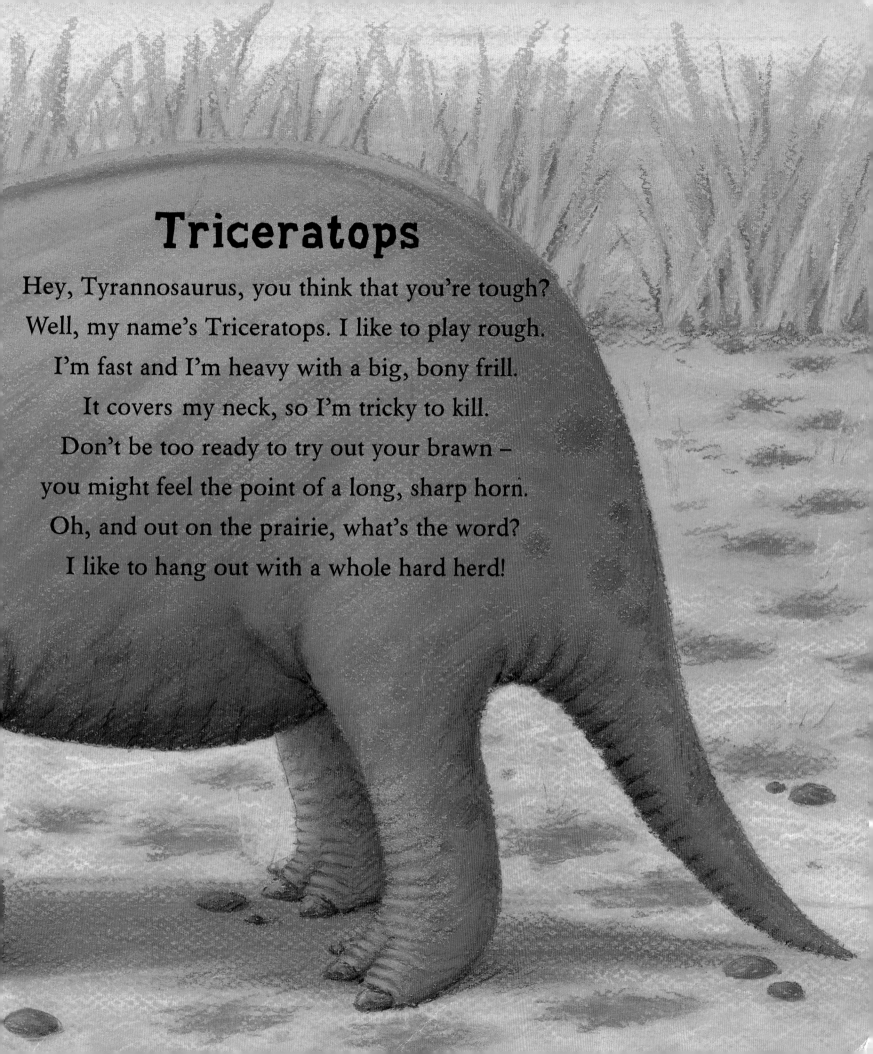

# Triceratops

Hey, Tyrannosaurus, you think that you're tough?

Well, my name's Triceratops. I like to play rough.

I'm fast and I'm heavy with a big, bony frill.

It covers my neck, so I'm tricky to kill.

Don't be too ready to try out your brawn –

you might feel the point of a long, sharp horn.

Oh, and out on the prairie, what's the word?

I like to hang out with a whole hard herd!

# Kronosaurus

I am big-head Kronosaurus, monster of the deep.
Gliding through the ocean, I doze but never sleep.
Fear me in the daylight, fear me in the dark,
fear me for I seem to be a prehistoric shark.
My jaws are really massive. My paddles give me speed . . . .

# Mononykus

Look at me. I'm Mononykus. What on earth am I?

A weird kind of dino-bird that cannot even fly.

My wings look like a ballet skirt, a funny mass of fluff.

They make me seem so silly – I wish that I looked tough.

I'd like to be a dinosaur but have to be a bird,

and with my beak and feathers – well, don't I look absurd?

# Deinonychus

We're the deinonychuses. We're ready to attack.
Watch us as we race along, running in a pack.

We're cunning, yes, we're clever, and we mean to get our prey.
We hunt it down together so it never gets away.

Our toenails are our weapons. Each one is like a knife.
So when you hear us coming,

## Pteranodon

was more like a glider than a bird!
It had a wing span of seven metres.

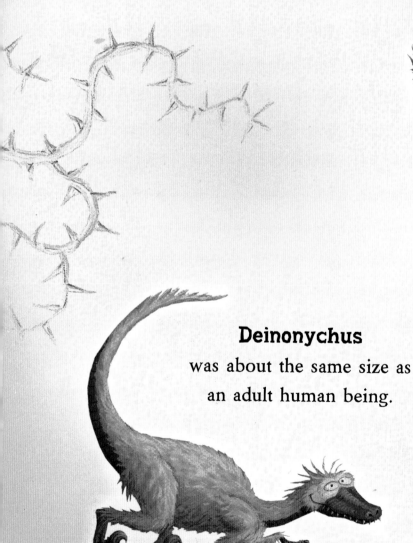

## Deinonychus

was about the same size as
an adult human being.

## Mononykus

had stumpy wings that were
no use for flying. It might have
used them to help it balance.

## Diplodocus

was one of the longest dinosaurs. At around 30 metres, it was roughly the length of three buses.

## Triceratops

means "three-horned face".

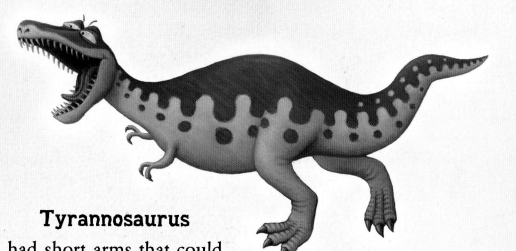

## Tyrannosaurus

had short arms that could grab hold of its prey but did not reach its mouth!

## Kronosaurus

was one of the biggest sea reptiles, with a head the same size as a large car.